UNDER *the* SAME CEILING

UNDER *the* SAME CEILING

Of Dust, Dreams and Dignity

Jasmine Meher

EXCELLER BOOKS®
A GLOBAL PRESS

Under *the* Same Ceiling
Of Dust, Dreams and Dignity

Cover by Exceller Books using resources from Pixabay.com

ISBN: 978-93-48892-03-4

Published in India in 2025 by Exceller Books,
An imprint of GE Group,
G1, Dream Apartment, Degree College Road, Belgharia,
Kolkata, 700056, India
www.excellerbooks.com

EXCELLER BOOKS®
A GLOBAL PRESS

To the Almighty

Contents

~ 1 ~

The Morning That Knows Every Secret

It began with the creak of the servant quarters' wooden door, the hush of a sari's pleats gathering around weary feet, and the splutter of the kitchen tap. The morning knew her first—Radha—the woman who stitched each day together before the world even opened its eyes.

She moved through the house like breath through silence—present, essential, unnoticed. Her fingers, rough like the earth after harvest, held the broom with practised ease. Every swish echoed a story she never told. Thirty-eight years of life had etched themselves into the folds of her sari and the slope of her shoulders.

Radha didn't speak much, not because she had nothing to say, but because words were a luxury she had long ago buried beneath survival. The house had become her rhythm—boiling milk at six, folding shirts at seven, scrubbing corners no one ever looked at. Each task a prayer, each silence a scream.

She rarely looked up the stairs, where dreams wore perfume and called her "Radha bai."
Upstairs, on the first floor, in a room draped in beige curtains and broken scripts, lay Maya.

The alarm hadn't gone off...again. Her phone blinked a missed call from "Casting Director New Delhi." Her pillow held smudges of last night's eyeliner, and her diary lay open with half-written lines:

"Do you see me? Or just the version you want to cast?"

Maya Mehra, twenty-six, aspirant of dreams she wasn't sure belonged to her anymore.

She sat up slowly, light spilling on her face through the window net. Her beauty was the kind that intimidated some and invited judgment from others—too polished for reality, too raw for fantasy. Her heart, however, was a battlefield of rejections and rehearsals. She had become a collage of headshots, tight smiles, and the constant sting of "we'll call you."

Downstairs, a kettle whistled. She barely heard it.

Radha was boiling the tea. Maya had long stopped noticing who did what in the house. Her world was full of lines to memorise and mirrors that didn't lie but never quite showed the whole picture either.

In the thin air between floors, their lives existed—one folding other people's clothes, one trying to fit into roles written by strangers.

The ceiling between them wasn't just made of concrete. It was built of silence, assumptions, and invisible boundaries. Yet, they both knew what it meant to be unseen.

One cleaned behind the mirror.

The other practised pain in front of it.

Neither knew yet how closely their stories would entwine. But that morning, something lingered in the air—an invisible thread pulled taut, waiting to be tied.

~ 2 ~

The Mirror and the Mask

Painted lips and borrowed lines,
She stands before a mirror of glass and doubt.
Every "yes" sounds like "maybe,"
And every "no" echoes failure.

Maya traced the outline of her reflection with her finger, the surface cold and smooth. The mirror didn't blink. It had watched her smile through brokenness, cry with lipstick still intact, and pretend to be someone she wasn't—over and over again.

Scripts lay scattered on her bed—marked, highlighted, and rejected. Today's audition was for a police officer in a regional OTT series. Yesterday, it was a young widow with "emotional depth" but not too much "baggage." She had learned to cry on cue, but it was harder to cry for real now.

Her room was messy—makeup palettes opened like wounds, costume jewellery entangled like her thoughts, and a half-eaten toast turning cold. The chaos was curated. It reminded her of her struggle, in case she ever forgot.

A knock at the door.

It was her mother.

"Maya, breakfast's ready."

"Not hungry," she called out, her voice flat, rehearsed.

She heard Radha's voice faintly downstairs—murmuring something, maybe a song in Odia, maybe just a reminder to herself. Maya had never really listened. In this house, listening wasn't encouraged—performing was.

She sat down at her dresser, dabbed some concealer under her eyes, and looked herself straight in the face. Not Maya, the daughter. Not Maya, the girl with dreams. But Maya, the product. The act. The *almost-there*.

She remembered the first time she stood on stage in school. The applause had wrapped around her like a warm hug. It had felt like love. Now, applause was just noise if it didn't come with an offer.

Scrolling through Instagram, she saw a former classmate had landed a role in a big-budget film. Hashtag "blessed." Hashtag "grateful." Maya's stomach turned—not from jealousy, but from the feeling of being left behind. She had talent. She had hunger. But neither paid the rent.

Downstairs, the dishes clinked. Radha was cleaning again. Same routine. Same rhythm.

Maya wondered, just for a second, if Radha ever felt this tired. Not body-tired, but soul-tired.

New Message: "Hey Maya, you didn't get the part. But we'll keep you in mind for future roles."

She didn't even flinch this time. Instead, she opened her diary, flipped to a blank page, and scribbled: "What does it mean to matter in a world that forgets so easily?"

Upstairs, she was invisible in a crowd.

Downstairs, Radha was invisible in solitude.

The ceiling stood between them—one carrying dreams, the other carrying dust—neither knew they were more alike than different.

~ 3 ~
Threads of Silence

Radha stood by the sink, her hands submerged in soapy water that had turned a tired grey. Her bangles clinked quietly, a rhythm as steady as her breath. Outside, the city buzzed—horns blaring, vendors shouting—but in this kitchen, there was only the hum of the refrigerator and the occasional sigh of a house trying to stay intact.

Maya sat on the dining table, scrolling aimlessly through her phone. Her plate, barely touched, held a piece of toast turning cold. Her mother had gone out for a temple visit. Her father was asleep after a night shift.

Just Radha. Just Maya.

Two women under the same ceiling.

Maya glanced up briefly. Radha didn't look at her. She never did unless spoken to. It wasn't fear—Maya had realised that long ago—it was conditioning. The kind that kept people in the corners of rooms even when the rooms were empty.

Radha wiped her hands on the edge of her saree and turned to leave.

"Radha Didi," Maya said, her voice softer than usual.

Radha paused mid-step.

"Yes?"

Maya hesitated. "Do you ever… feel tired of being here?"

Radha looked at her for a moment—really looked. Not at the actress, the daughter, the boss's girl—but at Maya, with messy hair and eyes that looked a little too lost for a house like this.

"Yes," she said simply.

And then, just as simply, she walked away to hang the wet cloth on the back balcony.

Maya didn't know why she asked. She wasn't used to speaking to Radha. It felt strange. Improper, even. But something about Radha's silence filled the room like truth.

And Radha—she wouldn't tell anyone, but that one word, that one moment of being asked how she felt—it curled inside her like a forgotten song remembered suddenly.

Maya's Reflection

Maya stood by the window, her gaze lost in the movement of the street below. The world outside was always moving. Cars honked, people hurried, and somewhere in the chaos, she felt small. The city had swallowed her dreams, chewed them up, and then spit them out as something else entirely.

She wanted to scream, to shout at the world for making her feel so insignificant, for reducing her to an almost-actor, an almost-daughter, an almost-woman.

She wasn't sure who she was anymore. The scripts had become a blur, and the roles she had hoped for seemed so far out of reach. But then, she thought of the mirror—of the mask she wore each day to face the world. A mask that was getting harder and harder to wear.

And yet, she kept trying. The hunger for recognition, for love, for something real—it gnawed at her.

Radha's life was a series of small, unnoticed acts. She worked, loved, and sacrificed in silence. Maya's life, on the other hand, was a loud battle against a world that seemed to hear only what it wanted to. They were like two parallel lines, always moving forward but never quite touching.

And yet, they both lived in the same house, breathed the same air, shared the same walls, but remained unseen—their stories untold, their pains unspoken.

As the sun dipped lower in the sky, their worlds continued to orbit, separate but intertwined. Radha, folding clothes; Maya, running lines in front of the mirror. Both lost in their own silent wars, unaware of the quiet resonance their lives shared.

~ 4 ~

Walls That Divide

The evening light stretched long across the walls, casting deep shadows. Radha stood in the kitchen, slicing vegetables with practised ease. Her hands moved quickly, rhythmically, as if she could cut through time itself—through the years of silent servitude, through the pain of all that had gone unsaid in her life.

She didn't notice when Maya stepped into the room. It wasn't that Maya had been quiet—it was just that Radha was lost in a world of her own, one where the sounds of chopping vegetables were the only symphony that mattered.

Maya, however, noticed everything. She saw how Radha's hands trembled ever so slightly as she reached for the onions, how she adjusted her sari without thinking, smoothing the wrinkles as if they were her own. The quiet between them felt heavy now, almost like a slow-pounding drumbeat in Maya's chest. She wanted to say something, anything, but the words didn't come.

Instead, Maya took a deep breath and broke the silence.

"Radha didi," she said, her voice soft, tentative.

Radha didn't stop chopping. She didn't even look up. "Yes?" Her voice, as always, was calm and measured, a reflection of a life lived in quiet endurance.

Maya stepped closer, her gaze fixed on Radha's movements. "Do you…do you ever think about leaving?"

It was a simple question, but for Radha, it felt like a thunderclap. She paused, the knife hovering mid-air, her breath caught in her throat. No one had ever asked her that before. Not seriously, not with the intention of listening.

She finally lowered the knife and placed it on the counter, turning to face Maya. For the first time in a long while, her eyes met Maya's—not with the indifference she usually wore, but with something more raw, something that made Maya falter.

Radha's voice, when it came, was quiet but firm. "Where would I go, Maya?"

Maya opened her mouth, but the words caught in her throat. She had never seen this side of Radha before—the side that carried not just the weight of her job, but the weight of a life lived in a system that never asked her opinion.

Radha turned back to her task, the knife resuming its steady rhythm. "No, I never think of leaving. I think of surviving. I think of providing. I think of seeing another day."

Maya stood there for a long moment, her mind racing. She had always considered herself someone who struggled. But here was Radha, a woman who had never been given the privilege of struggling against anything but her own limitations, her own survival.

Maya's chest tightened. The reality of their worlds, the walls that separated them—had she ever truly seen it?

Without another word, Maya turned and left the kitchen. Radha continued her work, but there was a weight in the air now—something had shifted, something small but significant.

Later that evening, as the house fell into a quiet lull, Radha sat outside on the small balcony, a cup of tea resting between her hands. She looked out at the sprawling cityscape, her eyes lost in the lights of the buildings that rose high into the sky.So much ambition in the world, she thought. So much desire to be seen, to be known. But no one sees me.

Maya, in her room, stood before the mirror. She had just come back from an audition, her hair frizzy from the rain, her spirits low. She stared at her reflection for a long moment, not recognising the girl looking back at her.

Who am I? she wondered. Who am I beyond this face, beyond this mask I wear for the world?

She took a deep breath and grabbed the script again, forcing herself to read the lines one more time.

But it felt hollow. The words were empty.

That night, as Radha slept in her small room and Maya lay wide awake, their worlds were closer than they had ever been—if only in the quiet understanding of shared loneliness. Two women living under the same roof, yet bound by invisible walls they could not name, yet could not escape.

Two lives, side by side,
Yet the walls between them stretch far and wide.
One dreams in silence, the other in loud despair,
But neither can reach the other's air.

It was a night like any other, with the moon casting its silver glow over the apartment. The house was quiet, save for the soft sounds of the city in the distance. Maya, in a rare moment of solitude, sat on the floor of her room, surrounded by scattered audition scripts and torn-up notes. Her nerves were on edge. She had just received another rejection. The weight of it all seemed too much—her dreams, her career, her unspoken fears.

Radha, meanwhile, was in the kitchen cleaning up after dinner, her steady hands moving through the motions she had perfected over the years. As always, she worked with precision, as if the rhythmic task could somehow calm the chaos in her mind.

It was then, out of nowhere, that the sound of glass breaking echoed through the silence of the apartment.

Maya had thrown her phone, in frustration, against the wall. The screen shattered into countless tiny pieces, scattering across the floor like fragments of her broken dreams.

Radha froze at the sound, her heart skipping a beat. For a moment, she thought it might be something else—a warning, a sign of something far worse—but she quickly gathered herself and went to Maya's room.

Maya sat on the floor, her hands trembling, staring at the broken pieces of her phone. It wasn't just the phone; it was everything. The pressure to succeed, the endless auditions, the constant feeling that she was never good enough—it all spilt over.

"I'm never going to make it," she whispered, her voice barely audible.

Radha stood at the doorframe, her eyes softening. She didn't speak right away. Instead, she crossed the room slowly, picking up the pieces of glass that had scattered, her hands moving with care.

Maya watched her, confused. She expected Radha to scold her, to tell her to stop being so dramatic. But instead, there was only silence.

Radha knelt beside her, her fingers brushing Maya's as she picked up the last shard of glass. There was something in her touch—a quiet understanding, a shared pain—that caused Maya's chest to tighten.

"Maya," Radha said softly, "it's okay to break sometimes. It's okay to not have everything figured out."

Maya blinked, her emotions rising to the surface. She had never heard Radha speak so openly, so vulnerably. Radha had always been the quiet one, the one who held everything in.

"Do you know what it feels like?" Maya whispered, her voice shaking. "To want something so badly, but no one seems to care? To keep trying and failing, and no one even notices?"

Radha paused, her hands stilling. Then, with a deep breath, she looked Maya in the eyes. "I know what it feels like to be invisible," she said, her voice steady but full of unspoken sorrow. "To give everything and be forgotten. To stay silent, because sometimes silence is the only thing you have left."

For the first time, Maya saw Radha—not as the domestic help, not as the silent worker in the background—but as a woman who had lived a life of her own, with her own dreams and disappointments.

The two women sat in the silence, the tension between them palpable, but something had shifted. It was no longer just about their roles in the house or the expectations placed on them. In that moment, they were just two women, struggling together.

The glass is broken, but the pieces remain,

Scattered across the floor of our pain.
We reach for them, we try to mend,
But some cracks never end.

Maya finally stood up, wiping her tears away. She didn't know what had just happened—why Radha had opened up to her like that—but she felt something within herself soften. It was as if the walls she had been so desperately trying to build between herself and the world had started to crumble.

"I'm sorry," Maya said, her voice raw. "I didn't mean to..."

Radha smiled, a quiet, understanding smile. "You don't have to apologise, Maya. We all break sometimes."

And for the first time in a long while, Maya believed it. They were not so different after all. Both were women trying to survive in a world that rarely saw them, both struggling with dreams that felt out of reach. And yet, in that moment, they had found a small fragment of peace in each other's presence.

This turning point shifts the dynamic between Radha and Maya, offering both women a moment of vulnerability and connection. It shows that, despite their differences, they share a common struggle. The walls that divided them began to break down, allowing them to see each other not as roles or expectations, but as individuals with real pain and real hopes.

~ 5 ~
Fractured Reflections

In the days that followed the night of the broken glass, things in the house felt different. The usual routine continued—Radha cooking, cleaning, tending to Maya's needs—but there was a new, unspoken understanding between the two women.

Maya had spent the next few days lost in thought, reflecting on the quiet conversation they had shared. It was almost like a shift had taken place in her heart. Her world, once full of ambition and competition, now seemed smaller, quieter. She had never considered how her drive for success had blinded her to the lives of those around her. Radha wasn't just a figure in the background. She was a woman, a person with her own dreams, her own life. And yet, Maya had taken her presence for granted for so long.

Maya couldn't stop thinking about Radha's words: "We all break sometimes."

She had always prided herself on being strong, on putting on a mask that convinced the world she was fine. But in Radha's quiet strength, Maya saw a different kind of resilience—one that didn't need recognition or applause. Radha's silence was not weakness; it was endurance.

Maya walked into the kitchen one afternoon, where Radha was preparing lunch.

"Radha didi," Maya said, her voice hesitant but filled with a softness she hadn't felt before. "Can I help you today?"

Radha looked up, surprised by the offer, but her face softened. She nodded silently and handed Maya the basket of vegetables. The two women worked side by side, neither speaking much, but the rhythm of their movements felt… different. There was no tension, no walls between them.

~ 6 ~
Echoes of Change

Maya's newfound empathy had begun to ripple out into her own life. The pressures of her acting career still lingered, of course. The rejections continued to come in, and the auditions still felt like a game of chance. But something had shifted inside her. For the first time, she didn't feel alone in the battle. Radha had given her something she hadn't known she needed—a kind of quiet solidarity.

One evening, Maya invited Radha to join her for dinner. It was a simple gesture, yet one that felt profoundly meaningful. They sat across from each other at the dining table, something that had never happened before.

"I've been thinking," Maya began, her voice soft. "About everything... about how much we take for granted. I don't even know if I can change anything about my career, but I want to make the effort. To stop running after dreams that don't make me feel…whole."

Radha looked at her, her expression calm but attentive. She had heard many people say things like that before—people who came to the city to make it big and then got lost in the pursuit of something that wasn't theirs to find. But she had learned to wait, to be patient, to let people find their way on their own terms.

"I don't know what your dreams are, Maya," Radha said, her voice steady, "but I hope you find peace in them."

Maya smiled faintly. "I'm beginning to understand that peace isn't something you chase. It's something you let come to you when you stop running."

~ 7 ~
The Silent Strength

For Radha, the days after their conversation had brought subtle but significant changes as well. She had always lived in the shadows, doing the work no one noticed. But something had shifted within her after hearing Maya's words. She realised that her life had been reduced to a series of chores, of expectations placed on her by society and others. She had never once considered what she might want for herself, beyond survival, beyond doing what was asked of her.

One afternoon, Radha found herself standing at the window, gazing out at the world. The city seemed so far away, but it had always been just a stone's throw from where she stood. The thought that she could have a life beyond this one—the idea that she could dream—was something she hadn't dared entertain before.

She had given so much of herself, but what if there was more to give? What if, after all these years, she could learn to take a step toward something for herself?

Radha didn't know what the future would look like. But for the first time, she felt that the world outside her small life was calling to her—not as a servant, not as someone invisible, but as a woman with her own strength, her own story to tell.

~ 8 ~
The Quiet Revolution

The changes in Maya and Radha were subtle at first—small gestures, like Maya making tea for Radha one morning, or Radha sharing a small secret from her childhood, a story about her village. But these moments added up, weaving a new kind of connection between them. They were no longer just two people forced to occupy the same space; they were beginning to see each other.

One day, when Maya returned from an audition, she found Radha sitting outside on the balcony, her face tilted toward the sun. Maya hesitated for a moment, then joined her.

"I've been thinking," Maya said quietly, "about how everything we do, we do because we have to. But maybe, just maybe, we can start doing things because we want to."

Radha didn't respond right away. She didn't need to. She simply nodded, her eyes meeting Maya's with a quiet understanding.

They both knew that the walls between them—though still present—were starting to crack and with every crack, the space between them grew smaller. Maybe, someday, those walls would fall entirely. But for now, it was enough to know that they were no longer invisible to each other.

~ 9 ~

The Stitch in Silence

It began with a small sound—tak tak tak—barely audible above the buzz of the city. Maya had returned early from an audition, her mind heavy with rejection, when she heard it. It wasn't the usual clatter of utensils or broom against tiles. It was rhythmic, focused. Curious, she followed the sound to Radha's small corner near the utility room.

Radha sat cross-legged on the floor, an old embroidery frame in her lap, fingers moving swiftly through colourful threads. The fabric told a story—tiny flowers blooming beside birds in mid-flight.

Maya stood stunned. "Radha didi…you made this?"

Radha glanced up, eyes wary. "It's nothing… just something I used to do, back in my village."

Maya crouched down beside her, truly seeing the work for the first time. The details were intricate, the colours alive. "This isn't nothing," she said softly. "This is art."

Radha smiled shyly, her fingers pausing. "I stopped when I came here. There was no time. No use for beauty when your hands are always washing someone else's dishes."

But Maya had already made up her mind.

~ 10 ~

A Canvas Opens

The next day, Maya brought home a small bundle of new fabric, threads, and a portable sewing machine. "If you can do this with scraps," she said, "imagine what you could do with more."

Radha hesitated. She wasn't used to this kind of attention. "Why are you doing this?" she asked.

Maya shrugged. "Because you deserve to be seen. And maybe I need to learn to see beyond myself."

They began spending evenings together—Maya helping Radha set up an online account to showcase her creations, taking photos of her embroidery, and reaching out to local artisans. With Maya's help, Radha's quiet art found its first admirers.

A local boutique offered to feature Radha's work. An NGO working with women artisans reached out for collaboration. Slowly, her name began to spread—not as someone's domestic help, but as Radha, an artist.

~ 11 ~

The Satisfaction of Silence

As Radha bloomed, Maya began to feel lighter. The noise of auditions, the sting of rejections—they still came, but they didn't sting as much anymore. Helping Radha reminded her of the why behind her art: to touch lives, not chase applause.

One day, Radha brought Maya a small gift—a hand-embroidered scarf with stars and wings. "For your next audition," she said, "may your dreams take flight."

Maya wore it to an audition for an indie film—the kind of raw, character-driven role she'd always dreamed of. This time, something clicked. A week later, she received a call...she had been selected.

~ 12 ~
A New Sky

Months passed. Radha's work was now being sold across cities. Maya's film premiered at a small but respected festival. Critics called her "a fresh, authentic voice." But when Maya stood on stage for her first award, she spoke not of fame or ambition, but of Radha.

"She showed me what real art is—patience, precision, and doing it with heart, even when no one is watching."

They returned home that night, not as employer and employee, but as two women who had changed each other's lives.

~ 13 ~

Two Names on a Doorbell

It had been a year.

The modest flat still stood the same, tucked into a forgotten corner of Mumbai—but the nameplate had changed.

"Maya Sen & Radha Mishra

Creative Studio – Dreams Rewoven"

They had started something no one expected: a tiny space where art met healing. Maya's rising fame opened doors, but she used it not to climb higher, but to bring others in. Radha's designs now travelled across borders. Each stitch told a story—of resilience, of womanhood, of things buried deep and unearthed with love.

They had become a quiet storm in the city—two women, two lives, one spirit.

~ 14 ~
A Scene within a Scene

Maya sat in a makeup chair, preparing for a scene that mirrored her own life—a woman finding her way after failure, helped by a stranger who becomes her soul mirror.

The director, who had discovered Maya through her indie film, whispered, "You've changed since the audition. There's something softer in your eyes now...something deeper."

Maya smiled. She knew what had changed. She wasn't acting anymore. She was living.

~ 15 ~

The Letter Radha Never Sent

One evening, while cleaning, Maya found an old notebook in Radha's drawer. Inside was a letter—unfinished, unsent:

"I never thought anyone would see me. Not really. I thought I was born to serve, not to dream. But you…you gave me a canvas. I don't know if I deserved it. But I know now… I want to live like I do."

Maya didn't speak of it. Instead, she wrapped it in silk and placed it in a frame beside Radha's latest embroidery—two hands, joined by a golden thread.

~ 16 ~
The Sky Opens

At a gala for women in art and cinema, Maya and Radha were invited as speakers. They stood side by side, the lights bright, but their hearts were calm.

Maya spoke: "Sometimes, the roles we play off-stage are the ones that save us."

Radha added: "And sometimes, the homes we work in…become the homes we build within."

The applause was not thunderous, but it was real.

The Ceiling That Was Sky
I once thought the ceiling held me down,
A world of limits, rules, and sound.
But now I know, it was just a disguise,
For the sky that waited beyond the lies.
You, who swept the floor in hush,
And I, who chased the world in a rush—
We found our worth not in applause,
But in the breaking of silent laws.

Under the same roof, we bloomed unseen,
Two stories stitched in golden sheen.
And now, wherever we rise or lie—
We live beneath a shared sky.